Doodlebug ELIZABETH

written by
Rachel Vail

illustrated by
Paige Keiser

Feiwel and Friends
New York

A FEIWEL AND FRIENDS BOOK
An imprint of Macmillan Publishing Group, LLC
120 Broadway, New York, NY 10271

Our books may be purchased in bulk for promotional,
educational, or business use. Please contact your local bookseller
or the Macmillan Corporate and Premium Sales Department at
(800) 221-7945 ext. 5442 or by email at MacmillanSpecialMarkets
@macmillan.com.

Library of Congress Cataloging-in-Publication Data is available.

ISBN 978-1-250-16222-9

Book design by Liz Dresner

Feiwel and Friends logo designed by Filomena Tuosto

First edition, 2020

1 3 5 7 9 10 8 6 4 2

mackids.com

To Judy Blume, my friend who saw me before she ever met me, and showed me that my feelings mattered. —R.V.

For my very good friend, Greg. —P.K.

Chapter
1

Class 2B is getting pets!

What pets?

I don't know.

Our teacher, Ms. Patel, said, "It will be a surprise when you come back after the weekend!"

I don't like surprises.

I like to know what to expect.

But I do like animals!

So I felt very excited and also very not.

Chapter 2

Our homework is:

Guess what animals we will host in Class 2B!

Draw a picture and write the name of the animals you think we'll have in Class 2B on Monday!

I love animals, and their names.

And drawing!

I got right to work.

Chapter
3

My first guess
is an elephant.
The name of this
elephant is Perry.

Chapter 4

My second guess is an owl named Daffodil.

Chapter
5

My third guess is
two jellyfish named
Frederika.

Chapter
6

My brother, Justin, says the name
we are supposed to put under the
animal is just the type of animal. Like
ELEPHANT or OWL or JELLYFISH.

"Ms. Patel said put their NAME," I
told him.

"The name of the animal," Justin said.

"Yes," I said. "And this stegosaurus is named Sassafras. She has the most stegs of any stegosaurus ever. And her stegs are made of glitter."

"Are you supposed to be using that glitter?" Justin asked.

Sassafras

"I am not taking questions at this time," I answered. "I am busy guessing what animals we will get in Class 2B."

"You're not getting a stegosaurus as a class animal," Justin said.

"Maybe we are," I said. "Maybe we're not. Stegosaurus is not my only guess. I have a lot of ideas."

"You might have to say good-bye to some of your ideas," Justin said.

"NO, I MIGHT NOT," I said.

I do not like saying *Good-bye* to my ideas.

I like saying *Hello* and *Have a seat would you like some cookies* to my ideas.

Chapter 7

A lot of kids guessed GERBIL or HAMSTER.

My best friend, Bucky, guessed LOBSTER.

Anna, who is my not-best-friend-at-all, guessed CAT.

Of course.

Anna loves only cats.

Mallory guessed TORTOISE, and her picture made everybody say *ooooo*.

It was a very cute tortoise Mallory drew.

Chapter

8

Nobody else did what I did.

They each had one drawing.

Even though Ms. Patel had said
animalS. With an *S* at the end.

They didn't write the animal's
name, just what type of animal.

I might have done
the homework wrong.

Again.

Chapter
9

Cali guessed it right.

BUTTERFLIES.

Her picture of butterflies had
wings that move.

Cali is very good at making things,
even though she is small and looks
like a kindergartner.

Her butterflies were much more beautiful than the real butterflies in Class 2B.

Chapter 10

The Class 2B butterflies don't look like butterflies at all.

They look like smudges.

Chapter
11

All my pictures of animals and their names got crumpled up.

I tried to be quiet, but crumpling is a noisy activity.

I shoved the crumpled papers in the garbage can while we lined up for recess.

"Elizabeth," Ms. Patel said. "Stay and chat with me for a minute."

Ms. Patel is very nice and beautiful.

She has mooshy gooshy arms and smile crinkles near her eyes.

I like to chat with her.

But if I am in trouble for making loud crumpling noises, maybe I would rather say good-bye to her, and go out to play instead.

Chapter

12

"Why did you throw all these wonderful pictures away, Elizabeth?" Ms. Patel asked.

I shrugged.

I didn't want to explain that I did it wrong.

Ms. Patel's long fingers smoothed my crumpled papers.

Her smile-crinkle eyes looked at each one.

"Ooo," she said. "I love Perry! What kind of animal is Perry?"

"An elephant," I said. "But we didn't get an elephant."

"Alas, we did not," Ms. Patel said. "What a fun class pet that would have been!"

"Yeah," I said.

"For us," Ms. Patel said. "Maybe not for Perry."

"Are you thinking about another animal for Class 2B?" I asked, very excited. "Did I give you ideas?"

"I love your ideas, Elizabeth," Ms. Patel said.

"I love my ideas, too," I said.

"Perry would need a different habitat than we could provide in Class 2B," said Ms. Patel.

"We could push the desks to the side," I suggested.

Chapter
13

"Maybe an elephant is a good animal to have as an *imaginary* class animal," Ms. Patel told me as we walked out to the playground together. "Some things we can't have in reality. But we can still have them in our imaginations!"

"I have two imaginary friends," I said.

"What fun!" Ms. Patel said.

"They aren't elephants. They are people. Their names are Mrs. Noodleman and Mr. Noodleman."

"What wonderful names," said Ms. Patel.

"Yes," I said. "I have one dog in reality named Qwerty, and one dog in imaginary named Spike. I also have an imaginary baby sister named . . ."

"Named what?"

"I don't know yet," I admitted. "I just imagined her up right now. Because I was thinking maybe you like imaginaries."

"I do," Ms. Patel said.

Chapter 14

When I got to the playground, all my friends crowded around me.

"Did you get in trouble?" Bucky asked.

I shook my head. "Just got a chat," I said.

"I had to stay inside for recess

once," Smelly Dan said. "I was in trouble."

"For pushing," Zora said.

"Yeah," Smelly Dan said.

"For pushing *me*," Jace said.

"Yeah," Dan said. It's not nice to call him Smelly Dan so I try not to, even in my mind. I sometimes forget to not.

"Well, you're in trouble now,"
Bucky said to me.

"Why?"

"Because, TAG! You're it!"

We all ran around playing tag
until it was time to go in and see
if our smudges had grown into
butterflies yet.

Chapter
15

Nope.

Still smudges.

The smudges are baby butterflies.

Caterpillars are kid butterflies.

I knew that already.

I just thought maybe baby

butterflies would have very tiny
baby butterfly wings.

Chapter 16

Everybody in Class 2B gets an
animal!

We were so excited, we had a dance
party about that news!

"We may have a misunderstanding,"
Ms. Patel said.

Misunderstanding means we are

excited but Ms. Patel is sorry because she wasn't telling the truth.

The animals we get are just in our minds.

But not imaginary.

Each kid of Class 2B gets to choose a real animal to learn about.

Then we will write an information report about our animal, and draw a picture of it.

It can be the animal you guessed, or another real animal.

Ms. Patel smiled at me.

I smiled back.

I think it was me who gave her this great idea.

"There are so many animals we are curious about, in Class 2B!" Ms. Patel said.

While we wait for the smudges to grow up, we will learn about butterflies, but also about other animals!

Chapter 17

Ms. Patel wrote our animal choices on the board.

"I want an antelope!" Zora yelled.

"I still want a cat!" yelled Anna. Because of course she did.

"I want a squid!" yelled Dan. "A squid can eat an octopus."

"I do NOT want an octopus," said Jace.

"I want a seahorse," yelled Mallory.

"Me too," Bucky said. "We could ride them together in the ocean!"

Ms. Patel wrote seahorse for Mallory and also wrote seahorse for Bucky.

Chapter

18

I slumped down in my chair.

I was feeling very sad, imagining
Bucky and Mallory riding seahorses
together through the ocean waves.

Bucky could have chosen lobster
again.

He didn't have to choose seahorse
with Mallory.

"Elizabeth?" Ms. Patel asked.
"Which animal would you like to
study?"

"A jellyfish," I said in my crankiest
voice.

Chapter
19

"Jellyfish," I told my family at dinnertime. "JELLYFISH!"

"You sure like saying jellyfish," Mom said.

"NO, I DO NOT!" I told her. "I DO NOT LIKE JELLYFISH AT ALL."

"So why did you choose jellyfish?" my brother, Justin, asked.

"I DON'T KNOW!" I yelled.

"Sounds like you feel a little disappointed with your choice," Dad said.

"NO, I DO NOT FEEL A LITTLE DISAPPOINTED!" I yelled, and sat under the table.

I did not feel a little disappointed.

I have never felt a little anything in my entire life.

I felt a BIG disappointed.

Chapter 20

While I slept, I dreamed about butterflies with no wings and jellyfish with frowning faces.

"Why are you such a frowny jellyfish?" I asked one, in the dream. "Are you a big disappointed, too?"

"Why don't you like us?" the jellyfish asked me back.

"I do like you," I said.

Some seahorses galloped by, with Bucky and Mallory riding them.

They were very beautiful.

I put my arm around the jellyfish. "I'm sorry, Jellyfish. I like you very much."

The jellyfish smiled huge at that.

"I like you very much, too, Elizabeth," said the jellyfish.

So when I woke up, I was happy about jellyfish.

Well, happier.

Chapter
21

Ms. Patel had more exciting news for us.

We are going to the library!

We had to walk in a line and be as quiet as our baby butterflies.

The new librarian, Ms. Robinson, said, "Welcome to the library, Class 2B!

"This is a magical place," she said.

"If you are curious about anything,
or if you just want to have fun and
stretch your imagination, you've come
to the right place!"

I was happy to hear we were in the right place!

"Some books are for information," Ms. Robinson said. "Some for imagination, and some? Combination!"

I think Ms. Robinson might secretly be a wizard.

Maybe there is sparkle dust in her hair.

Chapter
22

We looked and looked at information
books, deciding which we wanted to
borrow.

We had to find books with the
animals we chose, to get information
about them.

I found a book with a jellyfish on the cover, so I checked that out.

I put my name on the card.

My name is very long so it took two lines, even though I am one kid.

Mallory and Bucky were whispering together, looking at a book with seahorses in it.

Chapter 23

Every day our smudges are a little bigger.

They still do not look like butterflies at all.

They look like slightly bigger little smudges.

"Growing takes time," Ms. Patel said.

Chapter
24

Every day, the book about jellyfish
stays in my backpack.

It stays in at school.

It stays in at home.

It stays in on the bus.

My fancy paper for my information

report about jellyfish has no words or drawings on it except my name.

A lot of things take time.

Chapter
25

"I'm happy and sad today," I told
Gingy and Poopsie.

They are my grandparents and
also my babysitters when Mom and
Dad both are working at our
store.

"Mmm," said Gingy. "That happens to me sometimes, too. That feeling is called *ambivalent*."

"What does that mean?"

"Just what you said—feeling one way but also the opposite way."

"Well, to me that feels confusing," I said.

"To me, too," said Gingy.

"I feel snacky," said Poopsie.

"You always feel snacky," Gingy told him, and put some cookies and sliced apples on the table. "Elizabeth, what are you feeling ambivalent about?"

"Jellyfish," I said.

"Oh! No wonder," said Poopsie, with a cookie in each hand. "Jellyfish!

Pound for pound, jellyfish are the
most heartbreaking fish in the sea."

Chapter
26

Poopsie told me a long story about a jellyfish and a peanut-butter fish.

They fell in love because they were meant for each other, a perfect couple. But their families did not want them to get married.

"Why not?" I asked Poopsie.

"Exactly," said Poopsie. "There's no good reason to stand in the way of someone else's happiness!"

"Yeah!" I yelled.

"More happiness! More love!" Poopsie yelled.

"More happiness! More love!" I yelled, too.

"Woo-hoo!" yelled Poopsie.

"Woo-hoo!" I yelled, too. We made a protest parade, marching around with our fists in the air, yelling, "MORE HAPPINESS! MORE LOVE!"

"I'll write about peanut-butter fish and jellyfish in my homework and everybody will join our protest!" I yelled.

"More happiness! More love!" yelled Poopsie.

"Poopsie," said Gingy.

Poopsie sat down from our protest parade and looked bashful at Gingy.

Chapter 27

"Elizabeth," said Poopsie. "There's an extra detail in the tragedy of jellyfish and peanut-butter fish that I need to tell you about."

I sat down next to him. "Oh, good," I said. "Tell me."

I like getting a check plus and

a star sticker on my homework, so
I wanted to make sure I got all the
information right.

"Tell her the truth, Poopsie," said
Gingy. "You don't want Elizabeth to
get in trouble because of things you
made up!"

"The truth, okay," Poopsie
whispered, leaning close. "The big
reason the jellyfish's family didn't
want jellyfish to marry peanut-butter
fish is because peanut-butter fish is
imaginary."

I nodded.

"And jellyfish are real," he
whispered.

I nodded again.

"You understand?"

"That would make it hard to be

married to each other," I said. "Even if they really love each other."

"Yes, I knew you would understand," said Poopsie.

Chapter
28

I took my library book out of my backpack and showed it to Gingy and Poopsie.

"It has a lot of information," I said, opening it.

There were so many words on every page it was hard to pick one to start with.

The words looked like thousands of baby butterfly squiggles.

Gingy and Poopsie and I looked at those squiggles.

"I think this many letters on one page is too many," I whispered.

"It is a bit overwhelming," said Gingy.

"Well," I said. "I don't know what that word means, either."

"I bet you do," Poopsie said.

I decided to guess. Hm. *Overwhelming.*

"It sounds like, when you have to hurry in the bath so your dad pours water over your head to get the shampoo out. And it goes in your mouth and eyes. And you weren't ready so maybe you might cry. Is that *overwhelming*?"

"Yes," said Gingy. "That is a great description."

"Please show me the part here about the peanut-butter fish," I said. "I have to write three sentences and draw a picture by tomorrow. It's overwhelming."

Chapter
29

There was nothing in the whole library book about peanut-butter fish.

Information books don't include all the facts your Poopsie made up, apparently.

I tried to copy a picture of a jellyfish.

The picture in the book looked like this:

My picture looked like this:

My three sentences of writing homework are:

1. My animal is jellyfish.

2. Jellyfish have no brains!

3. That is a fact, not an insult to jellyfish.

I am also writing this bonus

sentence for extra credit, like maybe
a sticker of a star or a cute animal,
please, Ms. Patel:

4. Peanut-butter fish are imaginary.

Chapter
30

We have caterpillars! The baby smudges grew into kid stripey wiggles!

We are all very proud of them.

"Let's draw pictures of our caterpillars!" Ms. Patel said.

We love drawing in Class 2B!

We sat right down at our desks and started to draw.

"Hang on!" Ms. Patel said. "Drawing is not just making marks on a paper."

I thought that was what drawing is, so I was surprised at that news.

"Drawing," said Ms. Patel, "is more about looking closely."

She put the caterpillar net house on the floor.

"Come," Ms. Patel said. "Bring your papers and pencils."

We all crowded around the net house.

"Look closely," Ms. Patel said. "Choose one of the caterpillars."

I chose the cutest one.

"Draw what you are really seeing,"

Ms. Patel said. "Not just how you remember a caterpillar looks. Look closely and bring the image inside you."

I looked closely at my caterpillar and tried to bring the image of it inside me.

"How many ridges are there?" Ms. Patel asked us. "How thick is that stripe of yellow?"

The only sound in Class 2B was colored pencils scratching on paper, and eyeballs looking closely at caterpillars.

Chapter
31

My drawing looked a little like my
caterpillar.

Also a little like all the other
caterpillars.

But mostly like mine.

Mine is named Etiquette, I decided.

I think that's a name. It might be a word.

I heard it somewhere.

It can also be the name of my imaginary baby sister.

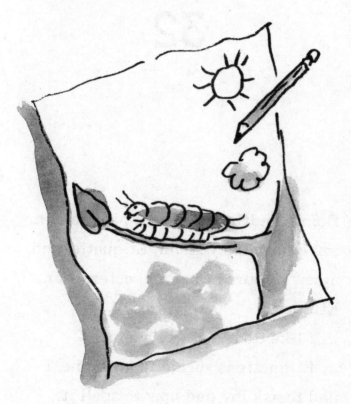

Chapter
32

Before bedtime, I drew a picture of my imaginary baby sister, Etiquette, and a new picture of my real caterpillar, Etiquette.

I like them both very much.

Etiquette is such a fancy name, I had to ask my dad how to spell it.

It took me a few tries to get it right.

So I hope my real caterpillar and imaginary baby sister are both up to it.

Edecat

Ettikit

Etiquette ✓

Chapter 33

Ms. Patel gave back our information papers about our animals.

Mine had a check plus! And a star sticker! And also a sticker of an elephant!

There was also a word in fancy writing.

It was very beautiful, up there on top of my page.

When it was time to pack up/stack up to go home, I asked Ms. Patel what her word said.

"Interesting!" Ms. Patel said.

I nodded.

"With a—the boinger on the end." I pointed at it. "This! For when you're excited."

"Exclamation point," Ms. Patel reminded me.

"I like those," I said. "They are my favorite kinds of points."

Chapter
34

I held my paper very proudly, the whole way home on the bus.

My best friend, Bucky, held his paper about seahorses very proudly, too.

I didn't look at it to see if he had stickers or the word *interesting* on his.

I was staying very proud and very happy of my jellyfish.

I didn't want to feel sad and mad and *why did you do seahorses with Mallory* instead.

Sometimes it takes a lot of hard work to stay happy.

Chapter
35

Our caterpillars shed their skin!

That is a normal thing for caterpillars to do.

No reason to panic about that.

It is not gross.

Even if it looks a little bit gross.

Kids don't shed their skin.

Ours can stretch.

We don't have to crawl out of our skin one Tuesday night and leave it on the floor like laundry and then wake up looking different.

That's just for caterpillars.

Don't worry.

Chapter
36

Sometimes we do have to
get new sneakers, though.

Chapter
37

"Cats larger than mountain lions don't purr," Anna said.

"Okay," I said. I was being Super Elizabeth on the swing, in my new sneakers.

Super Elizabeth doesn't care about cats.

"Cats never tuck their paws under themselves unless they're feeling safe," Anna said.

"Why not?" Bucky asked.

He was supposed to be Super Bucky, flying on adventures with me.

Not Regular Bucky, asking about cats and their feelings.

"In case they need to defend themselves," Anna said. "I did a lot of research for my information paper on cats. How do jellyfish defend themselves, Elizabeth?"

I thought about my jellyfish information paper.

There was nothing about defending themselves.

"Jellyfish go with the flow," I said.

"Cool," Bucky said.

"One time, the country Belgium tried to train cats as mail carriers," Anna said.

"Seriously?" Bucky asked, and stopped swinging. "That's amazing!"

"It went very poorly," Anna said.

"Good to know," I said. "Some jellyfish are deadly."

Chapter 38

"Drawing is not just making marks on a paper," I explained to Gingy. "We are learning how to really draw in second grade."

"I've always wished I knew how to draw," Gingy said.

"Lucky you!" I told her. "I will teach you."

"Great," Gingy agreed. She is a very good babysitter because she likes to learn.

"We can draw each other's faces!" I told her.

"Wonderful!" said Gingy.

"Look closely," I told her. "Draw what you are really seeing, not just how you remember I look."

"I'll try," Gingy said.

"I'll try, too," I said.

We looked and looked at each other's faces.

Chapter 39

Our pictures came
out very good.

We hung them
on the refrigerator
and let everybody
admire them.

Chapter 40

"What happened to Etiquette?" I yelled.

"What's wrong, Elizabeth?" Ms. Patel asked. "You're upset about . . . what now?"

"Etiquette!" I yelled, and pointed. There were no more wiggly

squiggly caterpillars in the net house.
Only greenish brownish lumps stuck
to the net wall.

Chapter
41

Ms. Patel called everybody to the net house and pointed. "Does anyone know what has happened to our caterpillars?" Ms. Patel asked us.

"They turned into poo?" asked Jace.

That made Dan laugh so hard.

"They DIED?" Mallory asked.

Mallory and I looked at each other with big, scared eyes.

"No!" said Anna. "They made their chrysalis."

"They made who?" asked Mallory.

"Chrysalis is a stage," said Cali. She has trouble with the letter *S*, so it sounded like *Kryth-a-lith ith a TH-tage*.

That sounded so cute everybody said *awwww*.

I wish I had trouble with the letter *S*.

Also that my name could be Krythalith instead of Elizabeth.

"The chrysalis stage lasts five to ten days," Ms. Patel told us. "They'll stay very still on the outside, while

inside, they are transforming
into . . . ?"

"Butterflies!" we yelled.

"Shhhh," Anna said. "We need to
let them have quiet, to transform."

"They won't mind a little
celebration, Anna," Ms. Patel said.
"It's okay."

Yeah, Anna, I said on the inside of
my imaginary chrysalis.

Chapter
42

Every day, we check our chrysalises.

Every day, not butterflies yet.

I couldn't even really tell which one was Etiquette, my favorite caterpillar.

"It's that one," I said to Mallory anyway.

"Amazing," said Mallory. "That's
the prettiest chrysalis, I think."

"Me too," I said. Then I whispered,
"She can be your favorite, too."

"Thanks," Mallory whispered
back, and then leaned closer to the
net house. "Good job transforming,
Etiquette."

Chapter
43

At drawing time, I drew a picture of me and Mallory both getting a ride on Etiquette, after she turns into a butterfly.

I wrote *Elizabeth* and *Mallory* and *Etiquette* under the picture.

Artists do that.

Grownup artists, even.

Not just kid artists in Class 2B in case people can't tell what the picture is of.

Elizabeth Mallory Etiquette

Chapter

44

"Cats would have made more interesting pets," Anna said.

We were looking at our chrysalises. The butterflies were still inside.

Every time Anna says *cats*, I want to yell, *Stop saying cats!*

I held that yell in.

I tried to think of something nicer
to say instead, something Super
Elizabeth would say.

"Or jellyfish could also be cool," I
said. "Or an elephant."

"I had a cat when I was a baby,"
Anna said.

"I have a dog," I said.

"My cat died. She was very old."

"Oh," I said.

"I didn't even get to say good-bye to
her."

"Why not?" I asked.

"I didn't know how to talk," Anna
said. "I was a baby, remember?"

"That's a good reason," I said.

"I don't remember her," Anna
whispered, frowning. "I wish I could
at least have said good-bye."

Anna is not my best friend.

I put my arm around her anyway.

"We could draw a picture of your cat, so you can remember her," I said. "And then you can say good-bye, or hello, or whatever you want to say to her."

"But how can we draw her?" Anna asked. "I can't look at her. And I don't remember how she looked!"

"We can look in our imagination," I said. "And then we can remember that."

I'm not sure if that is a way to draw, but it was my only idea.

"Okay," Anna said. "I think that's called doodling."

"I know that," I said.

I did not know that, but I hate when Anna knows more than I do.

We doodled so many pictures.

They were all of her cat whose name was Winsome.

We don't know what Winsome looked like so we doodled lots of options.

Chapter
46

I let Anna take home all the pictures
we doodled.

I don't like saying good-bye to my
artwork, especially when my mom
hasn't seen them yet so she will never
look at them and say, "Beautiful,
Elizabeth!"

But Anna looked so happy with
all the doodles, it felt okay to say
good-bye to them.

Not even ambivalent, really.

Chapter
47

The butterflies are trying to poke out of their chrysalises!

It is disgusting!

It is also exciting, in a slow-motion way.

Smelly Dan stood right next to me.

We were all looking at the net house.

"Butterflies are my second-favorite bugs," he said.

"They aren't bugs," I said.

"Actually, Elizabeth, they are," Anna said.

What I didn't say was:

Actually, Anna, remember how nice I was to you about your dead cat yesterday?

What I did say was:

"Ms. Patel, are butterflies bugs?"

"Great question," said Ms. Patel. "Butterflies *are* insects."

"See," said Anna.

"But they are not technically bugs," Ms. Patel added.

"See," I said back to Anna.

Chapter
48

Ms. Patel explained the difference between insects and bugs to us.

I didn't listen.

That topic was never very important to me and I still don't care.

Instead I just really looked at the butterflies and their new wings.

I knew they were going to come out
of there with wings.

I expected it.

That's what they do!

But also, it seemed like
imagination.

Or maybe like magic.

They are so beautiful.

Chapter
49

WHAT?!

We have to say GOOD-BYE to our butterflies?

Tomorrow we will take them outside and set them free.

We waited so long to say hello to our butterflies.

I do not want to say good-bye to them.

I felt a huge sad, all afternoon.

Chapter
50

Mom said the butterflies will fly away
and be happy.

It will be wonderful for them.

"But it won't be wonderful for
ME!" I said.

"I know," Mom said. "Sometimes
it's hard to watch someone you love

grow and change, and test her wings.
But it's also right and good, and a
very happy thing."

"I am NOT happy," I said. "I'm
overwhelmed! I'll never see Etiquette
again, forever!"

I hardly got to know our butterflies.

I'm actually not even sure which one is even Etiquette, my favorite butterfly.

That's why I had to cry.

Forever is a long time to not see your favorite butterfly.

Mom's hand on my back was warm and nice.

So was her idea, when I finished crying and used a tissue!

Chapter 51

Instead of taking the bus to school, I went in the car with Mom.

We wanted to get me there early.

I was the first kid in the classroom!

I opened my backpack and showed Ms. Patel what I had made.

Pictures and pictures of our butterflies.

Having adventures.

Playing with us.

Being happy.

"I'm feeling ambivalent about saying good-bye to our butterflies," I told Ms. Patel.

"Ambivalent!" Ms. Patel said.

"It means feeling opposite ways at the same time," I explained.

Ms. Patel nodded.

"I'm happy they will have freedom. And I'm sad that we'll never see them again."

"Except in our memories," Ms. Patel said.

"And in my doodles," I said.

"Yes," Ms. Patel said. "You've given me another great idea, Elizabeth!"

"I give her a lot of great ideas," I explained to Mom when she gave me a kiss good-bye.

Chapter
52

The whole Class 2B spent the morning doodling our butterflies and giving them advice.

"Find good flowers!" Cali said.

"Don't crash into windows!" said Dan.

"Float on breezes," Bucky
suggested.

"Drink yummy nectar!" said Anna.
"And look for cats!"

"Stick together," said Mallory.

"Don't forget us," I whispered.

I looked closely at each of them and drew them my best.

They are not bugs. But I am, I decided. A doodlebug.

I think that is a word but I am not sure so I kept it inside my imaginary chrysalis.

Chapter
53

It was time to take the butterflies outside.

We left our doodles in Class 2B and went out to the field, under the big tree.

Ms. Patel opened the net house.

Two of the butterflies flew right out, up into the sky!

Then another, and another, and another!

Until there was only one left in the net house.

I think it was Etiquette.

Chapter
54

I knelt down next to the net house and whispered to Etiquette.

"I know it's scary, Etiquette, and you probably feel ambivalent. But you can do it. You'll see. And I'll remember you forever. And any time you want, you can remember me!"

I think that helped her.

Because after I finished whispering, Etiquette flew out, and across the field.

She landed on a bush and flapped her wings a few times.

She was waving good-bye to me, I think.

I waved good-bye back.

And then she flew away.

Chapter
55

We were allowed to play outside even though it wasn't recess time!

We tried running around.

But what we were feeling was: not so playful.

We were feeling a big sad and a big proud.

And a lot of other big feelings.

So for a few minutes we all just sat together on the grass and looked at the sky.

Acknowledgments

With thanks and love to:

Amy Berkower, Elizabeth's wise friend and defender (also mine)

Elizabeth's best friends at Feiwel & Friends:

Anna Roberto, Elizabeth's new superhero

Liz Dresner, designer of the beautiful cover and interiors

Starr Baer, star of the schedule/copyediting/proofreading

Molly Brouillette, who sends me and Elizabeth to new horizons

Kim Waymer, who makes the actual book appear

Melissa Croce, who gets Elizabeth to libraries and schools, some of her favorite places

Liz Szabla and Jean Feiwel, steering Elizabeth toward her future

Paige Keiser, capturing the magic in the doodles

Carin, Meg, Lauren, Susannah, Stacy, Jill, Lynn, Stef, Melissa, Tania, Mary—treasured friends and fellow-travelers

Zachary and Liam, who grow and change, which is hard but wonderful; who bravely said good-bye to each butterfly and still say hello to each idea

Nina, who has also never felt a little anything in her entire life, either

Hannah, Emily, Isaac, Adam, Jon, Claudia, Sarah, Katrina, Bex, Simon, Syd, Simone, Jason, Stephen, Pen, Xan, and other pals who share their hilarious stories with me including emergency weird cat facts and other necessities

Nana & Papa, who know from love and art

Mom and Dad, unafraid of big feelings; you are my rock and my best cheering section

Jon, who still loves stories, and Kathryn, who makes Jon happy, which is the happiest thing for me

And most of all Mitch, forever and ever and ever

Thank you for reading this Feiwel and Friends book.

The Friends who made

possible are:

Jean Feiwel, Publisher

Liz Szabla, Associate Publisher

Rich Deas, Senior Creative Director

Holly West, Senior Editor

Anna Roberto, Senior Editor

Kat Brzozowski, Senior Editor

Alexei Esikoff, Senior Managing Editor

Kim Waymer, Senior Production Manager

Erin Siu, Assistant Editor

Emily Settle, Associate Editor

Rachel Diebel, Assistant Editor

Foyinsi Adegbonmire, Editorial Assistant

Liz Dresner, Associate Art Director

Starr Baer, Associate Copy Chief

Follow us on Facebook or visit us online at mackids.com

Our books are friends for life.